Also by Craig Rodgers

The Ghost of Mile 43
One More Number
Drift
Francis Top's Grand Design
Oriel
Twenty Ponds
Moonbeams
Clutch 1900

Francis Top's Lost Cipher

Stories by Craig Rodgers

Francis Top's Last Cipher is published in the United States of America by Death of Print, an alter ego of Malarkey Books, with the tacit permission of the Francis Top estate. Craig Rodgers, the author, maintains all rights to the stories within this book, no matter what Francis's long lost, fame-seeking relatives may claim.

Image on the cover courtesy of Everyday Basics on Unsplash.

ISBN: 979-8-9903240-3-9

©2024 Craig Rodgers

Table of Contents

Partygoers, Oil on Canvas, 1672	7
Dead Will Grow	10
At Night	15
My Lucky Day	16
Odds of Life	28
The Town's New Church	30
Custody of a Relic	33
Hemingway	47
The Latest Model	49
Thomas Is a Liar	54
Wrong Number	55
Two Inches of Tape	59
Some Trouble Next Door	61
Whisper to Trumpet	63
The Dream Hotel	65
Comes the Sorrower	68
Romance Novel	70
The Room in the Desert	91

PARTYGOERS, OIL ON CANVAS, 1672

The painting was perfect, everyone agreed.

"It's all so lifelike," said the confessor.

"Oh there I am," said the eunuch.

"It's fine," said the herald.

They stood gathered with their drinks and cheeses, staring, chatting, each in turn slathering on their own version of praise. It was the steward who first broke the spell.

"I don't see myself."

The painter looked at the painting and at the man and back again.

"You must've come in late, I'm so sorry. I'll fix it right away."

"You needn't do that. I was here the whole time, but it's already complete."

"I'm sure I would've seen you."

And.

"It's no trouble."

The steward's mouth opened and closed. He nodded and moved away, absorbed into the crowd. The painter brought out his tray with its many dabs of color, and he moved close to the canvas and he squinted, and then he went to work. Brushing along tender lines to recreate the idea of a moment. Then.

"What do you think?"

"That's very well done," said the steward.

"Captured perfection," said the confessor.

"Wait, where have I gone?" asked the eunuch.

"I needed the space. The body. For the steward."

The eunuch looked to the steward, who only smiled. Then came the fool. And the fool touched the eunuch's belly, and he spoke of the eunuch taking space, and the crowd they all laughed.

"Fix it," said the eunuch.

"What?"

"Fix it!"

The room's chatter fell hushed, and in its place came whispers. Somewhere on the other side of the room the duke spoke up.

"What's this now?"

"The painter. He's chosen to slight the court."

"I did not."

"He's insulted me and he's insulted us all."

Partygoers moved aside as through their assemblage the duke came. He passed among them with an easy smile that he soon turned on the painter.

"Is that true? Have you insulted the court?"

"I only paint what I see."

The duke took the painter by the shoulder and he squeezed and then patted there.

"That's no problem at all. Just paint what is, not what you see."

He gave the painter a shake and turned away.

The painter looked at the painting. He leaned back and cocked his head to the side. He pulled a glass of wine from a tray and drank it down. He looked hard into the painting and he drank another wine. Then he began to paint once more.

Some minutes went by and they began to gather. The confessor stopped to watch. The herald saw and with a grin moved on. Others couldn't believe. In their ones and twos they were pulled in to see. It was the fool who began to laugh. Others soon joined, and the duke was there again, moving through the parting crowd and turning his smile upon face after face. He saw the painting and the smile fell away.

"What are you doing, painter?"

There had been a shuffling. Where the duke had been now the form of the eunuch stood straight, and though the fool's body had been unaltered, the likeness of the duke was now clear upon his shoulders.

"If this is a joke we are not laughing."

The fool went on snickering but the crowd's laughs had otherwise died. The duke leaned close and spoke only for the painter to hear, and then he again turned and was swallowed by the party.

All whispers now. The eunuch sat with arms folded. The steward watched the eunuch. The herald left altogether. The painter drank more wine.

The confessor touched the painter's arm and they spoke in some confidence for a time. Then the confessor moved on, and the painter let his eyes move over the world of canvas, he looked and he closed his eyes and he opened them and looked again. He drank more wine. Then he began to paint.

Wild arcs of orange and black moved along the scene. What once had been carefully articulated moments in time were obscured by splashes of chaos brushed across their finities. Someone in the crowd gasped and someone else let out a moan and they again brought the duke forward, but the painter did not stop his thrashing additions as the duke spoke, and when his shoulder was held he pulled away, and when the duke told him coldly to paint what is, paint this and not what you see, the painter turned to him, and taking hold of a candle and touching its flame to the canvas smeared in oils he said I am.

DEAD WILL GROW

The grieving do not linger. Cousins, friends. They step close and nod in wordless prayer and move from this place and this moment onward to the rest of what existence offers up. Draped in black, these bereaved. They trickle away as the show goes on until in time the surviving brother is there alone, the last left to observe, the last to heave in quiet with some inner sorrow.

He speaks whispered words and then he only stands. Not thinking, not feeling. Breath falters with chest tight. He coughs, he clears throat. He wipes the sleeve of a hooded sweatshirt across his eyes. He nods some unspoken accord.

The retreat of cars has faded. The Lake Oriel Township Cemetery is a quiet place. He wants to sit but he does not. He lets his feet take him, he wanders with no aim deeper into aged rows of the dead.

The names carved in old stone ring familiar, townies going all the way back. Arthur Top. Frederick LaRue. The distant kin of someone who long ago mattered. Years tell their own tales. This man died in the war, this in the flu. Some go back and back more, no clear sense to the why of their arrangement.

The surviving brother drifts among markers faded and plots overgrown. He touches names now weathered beyond reading. He trods ground occupied by brush obscuring grave and walking path both.

He walks. Memories spiral. Tears again well in eyes and he goes on. He does not see the woman until his trek has brought him near collision. He gasps, he says I'm so sorry.

She looks away nodding. Older, gray hair unspooled and flowing. She holds the hem of her sundress in one hand and a half gone bottle of some dark liquor in the other, sloshing with an arm's swing in each step. She walks on feet bare.

The brother watches her go. He tries to offer some last declaration but the words don't come. Still he waits, bound to this place until she has altogether gone.

The grounds grow thicker still. More than unkempt. Pillars of remembrance fallen and left, moss overgrowing the etched tale of the lost. He navigates these forgotten dead until in his wandering a space opens of spare ground and there sits a stranger on a bench of old iron. In the man's hand is a yellowed and tattered paperback, from which he looks up but briefly. An old pulp number. A man on the cover, a cowboy on his knees. The reader on the bench wears a suit of black or dark blue. A purple bowtie hangs just off kilter. At his side sits the remains of a sack lunch in part consumed. Sandwich, pickle. He licks a finger and turns a page. He does not look up as he speaks.

"Sitting is an option, if you'd like."

The surviving brother sits. He wipes at his face and leans back.

"Did you lose somebody?"

The stranger shakes his head.

"Just visiting"

The surviving brother nods. He leans forward again, looking to the ground, the slow amble of bugs upon their way. Breeze touching flesh, trees dancing.

"I lost someone. It doesn't feel real."

The stranger makes a noise, a hum of assent or just having heard. He turns another page.

"My brother was a good man. He did his best. He tried to."

The stranger clears his throat with a pronounced churn, wet, very nearly a cough. He folds the corner of a page and closes his cowboy novel and in his lap he holds it in two hands.

"All our brothers do their best," he says, "and all our brothers fail. I'm sorry for your loss."

The brother looks to the stranger's face. He watches what he sees there, looking for something behind the words. The stranger looks out at the overgrown plots of those laid to their forever rest and holds his book in his lap. In time the brother nods.

"Did you see that woman?"

"Oh yes," says the stranger. "She comes to visit the older ones."

Trees move in the touch of breeze pushed along by some storm still miles off, limbs bouncing under its coming. The stranger watches their sway. He turns the paperback over facedown.

"The older parts of the cemetery don't get a lot of visits anymore, but the ones who come are the faithful still."

"The cemetery goes back in there? I ran into her coming out of the trees."

"The trees were here a long time before the cemetery. The old families planted them along with their dead."

"There's something lovely about that." "What."

"Growing trees from their loss. Life from life."

"That's a way to look at it."

"Is there another way to look at it?"

"The old families said a tree would sprout from the soul, and that soul would be bound to the earth for the life of the tree. There is a world where that is a lovely thought indeed. There is also one in which this looks an awful lot like they're trapping the dead so the living may haunt them still."

"Jesus."

"What."

"That's bleak."

The stranger shrugs.

"They're just stories the old families tell."

"What about you? What do you think?"

"What do I think about the trees?"

"About death."

"Oh. I think it doesn't matter what I think. What do you think?"

"I think death isn't what we think."

"That's probably good enough."

"And the trees?"

"The trees. I think the trees make for a nice story. I think that's why they planted them, and it's why some still come to them now. And maybe they believe, and for some it's to visit and remember the ones who were here before, and for some it's maybe something uglier. Something mean. But it's the intent that matters. For the ones who planted them, and the ones who come still."

"Like any grave."

"If you think so."

"Do you think if I plant a tree on my brother's grave his soul will grow in it?"

"I think it's okay if you believe it."

Winds rise, trees now leaning away from that touch.

"The sky looks wrong."

"This storm. Being gone before it comes is advisable."

The stranger takes his cowboy paperback and he tucks it away somewhere in his suitcoat and his trash he stacks and in its paper sack he rolls it until it is tight in one hand. He says I am sorry. About your brother. He says again don't linger here. Then he is standing and going and across the field of unkempt growth he fades and is gone.

The surviving brother stands. He moves along the treeline in deep grasses, past the cracked epitaph of somebody once loved, past some name sanded away by years. He comes to a hollow leading back into trees bent in rough oval, a path worn by those who come to this place, a doorway into time. He stands in that spot, listening to the gentle swish of a thousand thousand leaves, whispers of a faintest suggestion. A darkness gathers above.

AT NIGHT

The clock reads 2:04. The bedroom door is closed. He stares. He closes his eyes.

He opens his eyes. The clock reads 2:09. The bedroom door is open. He closes his eyes. He opens them. He stands and reaches out and he closes the door. He gets back into bed. The clock reads 2:11. He closes his eyes.

He opens his eyes. The clock reads 2:36. The bedroom door is open. He stands and pads his slow way through blue dark to a bathroom at hall's end. He urinates with eyes closed. He returns to the bedroom, one hand shutting the door behind him. He closes his eyes.

He opens his eyes. The clock reads 2:43. The bedroom door is open. He stares. Brow furrows. He leans and reaches and without getting up he pushes closed the door. He stares another moment. He closes his eyes.

He opens his eyes. The bedroom door is open. He sits up in bed, throws legs over the side. His feet touch cold floor. He stares. He pushes the door closed. He waits. The clock reads 2:49. The clock reads 2:50. The bedroom door is closed. He curls his form back into bed. He stares. The clock reads 2:53. His eyes fall closed.

He opens his eyes. The bedroom door is open. The clock reads 2:59. He stares. He stares. The clock reads 3:01. He pushes closed the door. He stares. The clock reads 3:05. The clock reads 3:08. He stares. The bedroom door is closed. He stares. The clock reads 3:15. He stares. The clock reads 3:30. The bedroom door is closed. He stares. He stares.

MY LUCKY DAY

Headlights push through country miles of dark. He cruises by the lights of the mine camp, and past the mill, and then for some time the old Chevrolet cuts through minutes of empty night. He rolls the dial and a big band number zings, he turns it up to a roar, and the cursory fall of raindrops is drowned out by the onslaught of song. He bops, he nods his head to the beat. He yawns.

An aberration appears ahead among the road's stretch of nothing. It is a glint of metal and then it is a hulk in the dark and as it nears it does resolve into the shape of a car stalled at its awkward cant in the ditch.

He pulls alongside and parks. He steps out into hot night. Raindrops fall and splash, some distance between each. He shields his eyes, he squints.

"Hot damn, but you've got a mess."

The man standing shadowed at the car's front steps around the fender and he says yes, he says I sure do.

"Could you give me a lift just into town?"

"It'd be unchristian not to."

"Well hell."

"You need to stow your gear there? Anything you leave out along the road, somebody's liable to come along and grab it."

The man turns back to the car. Rainfall thumps in its slow way. His back turned. He shifts his hat in place. When he turns again he is smiling.

"I've got my briefcase. That's all I need in the world."

Bruised dawn breaks as they pull into town. A weak blue film stretches across the surface of all things, light once again asserting itself. The town is a quiet place. Streets lay emptied of life. A light pops on here and there behind some window or other, the very first to begin again.

"Can you stop off up here? I need to make a call."

Downtown is a line of old wood storefronts whose foundations were laid down long ago by pilgrims too tired to go one step nearer whatever dream propelled them this far from grace. Offices, shops. Signs rest in dark, awaiting the onset of day.

They park and sit and the car ticks with pent intention. The traveler turns in his seat. He says well.

"Hang tight, I'll only be a minute."

He slams the door as he goes. Then silence. Stillness. The driver shifts in his seat. Moments and then minutes. The hue of every surface adjusts with morning's progression.

The briefcase waits on the floor. A lump of a thing, beaten in its journeys. Scuffed and bent and worn. He reaches and drags it into the seat. The latches are worn leather tongues. He turns. Across the street nothing moves. The drugstore window leaks a pale illumination.

A bell tinkles above as the door is pushed open. He steps into dayglow buzz. Colors vibrant march along shelves, an array of offers packaged or jarred and displayed in a parade of wants. Peanuts, gum. Baseball cards.

"Colonel?"

A door stands open behind the counter. A hole in the light. From there a man does come. Graying of beard and hair. A smock drapes his solid frame.

"Henry. By God, you're in early. We're open but not a thing is put away just yet."

"Colonel, did that man who came to use your phone already finish up?"

"Come again?"

"The man. I'm sorry, I don't know his name. He came in for the phone."

"Henry. Hey. I don't know what to tell you. I've been in and out of the back but. Hey. You're the only person who's been in yet."

He breathes through his nose, Henry does. He looks left and right, as if the traveler might be there, misplaced somewhere among the rows.

"Henry?"

"Thank you, Colonel. I must've been mistaken."

―――

They call it a diner but it isn't. It's a bar with a fry cook handy. Breakfast drunks hunch across the counter, red-eyed and yawning. Mother Judie mans the front. She gabs about whatever to whoever between burger flips. She sips dark liquid from a jar when she runs out of words. Sometimes her sips are deep gulps.

"Jude, hey."

"Henry. Morning."

"Is Cliff around?"

"Well Henry, that'd be a yes and a no. Cliff was out drinking with his brothers until just about sunup, and as it's now only a moment or two into the new day I'd give even odds that he's dead drunk and very asleep in my office. That may not fit the bill as far as 'around' goes, but it'll have to do."

"Thank you, Jude."

"You gonna wake him up?"

"I think I might have to."

"I apologize for the state you find him in."

"It's fine."

"You're a good boy, Henry."

Henry says thank you again.

The office is a cavern of barrels and shelves and crates lit by a scatter of lamps separated so that their touch illuminates only the suggestion of things. A sofa sits pulled into a far corner. On it snores a large man, wrapped in a tangle of sheets. Henry sets the briefcase down on the concrete floor. He touches the man's shoulder and presses there.

"Cliff? Cliff, hey."

The man coughs and huffs and rises to sit. He does not open his eyes. His hand rests on his knee and anchors there as moments of long breaths do come.

"Henry."

"I hate to wake you."

"What time is it?"

"Morning. I don't know. Cliff, something's happened."

"Did Judie send you back here to rouse me?"

"She said you were out drinking all night."

"She exaggerates."

"She didn't send me. She didn't want me to bother you."

"Well bother me you have. Something happened? What happened?"

"I picked up somebody thumbing a ride out by the mines."

"Weirdos out there."

"He seemed okay. Workaday suit and tie. Had an engine go bad on him."

"This fella have a name?"

"I didn't think to ask."

"Okay. Then what?"

"I don't know."

"What."

"He wanted me to pull up by Gregory's so he could use the phone. I waited a while but he didn't come back."

"He didn't come back."

"Yeah."

"And you waited."

"Yeah."

"Henry, come on."

"Well. I don't know what to do."

"The guy. He called whoever he needed to. He probably hotstepped it to wherever thirty seconds after you dropped him off."

"Cliff, I hear you."

Henry huffs, he looks around with a contained wildness. He reaches at his back and scoots to his front the traveler's briefcase.

"Something is very wrong."

He pulls the straps and the briefcase falls open with piles of currency displayed in its unhinged assortment. Some bundled, some not. All manner of denomination.

Cliff's eyes open and they widen. He sits forward.

"Well. That his?"

"He left it."

"Someone will come looking for that."

"I know."

"They'll hurt you if they find you with it."

"Cliff, I know."

Seconds of quiet. Cliff puts a hand to his face and presses there. Then he is standing and on bare feet he crosses the room. He says wait. Then he is gone. He's gone for some minutes. When he returns he carries two mugs. Steam rises. He hands one to Henry. The other he sets on a table. He takes a bottle of some unlabeled hooch and tips it into the mug. The bottle glugs twice, three times. He holds it up, he waggles it before him. Henry shakes his head no.

"Don't tell Jude."

Cliff sips this concoction and then he takes a deeper drink. He swirls it in his cup.

"Okay. Begin again. You picked up a guy thumbing out by the mines."

"I picked him up. His car was in the ditch."

"Then what?" "We drove into town."

"Did he say anything? Did he have anything with him besides the bag?"

"Just the case, that's it. We didn't do much talking, not that I recall."

"And he needed to use the phone."

"He pointed at Gregory's, he asked could I wait a minute. So I did."

"What did you do while he went in?"

"Far as I can tell he didn't."

"Didn't what?"

"Go in."

"How do you figure?"

"After I got done waiting I went in myself. Gregory was setting up. Said nobody'd been in but me."

"You think he could've missed him?"

"The colonel told me he'd been in the back, but I just don't see it. That old man doesn't miss much."

"Okay. Then what?"

"Then what? Then nothing. I opened the briefcase, I damn near fainted, then I came here."

Cliff lowers himself onto the sofa. He sips, he swirls. Somewhere a bell dings, someone's breakfast order now ready.

"Well. You gotta put it back."

"What?"

"In the car. The guy's car. You've gotta drive out there and put the bag back."

"But. Why?"

"Well you can't keep it."

Henry looks around. He turns his eyes to the floor.

"Henry."

"I thought maybe you could call around. If somebody's looking for it, maybe we get ahead of it. Maybe get a reward."

"Henry."

"You know some guys."

"I know some guys who play cards. I don't know the guys who know those guys. Not the ones you're talking about."

And.

"Henry. Put the bag back in the car."

"What are you going to do?"

"Sleep. I'm going to sleep."

———

The rain comes hard now. A bombardment unending. He drives along country miles sloshing between swamped pastures but when he comes to the mines he's passed no abandoned car. He turns around and drives slower now, braking for each fallen tree or lump of rotting hay, but when he arrives again at the outskirts of town he has passed no lost car and along the road he's seen not a soul.

Streets lined with little houses dipped in blues and yellows lead on until he finds himself parked at a curb. Home. Rain pounds the car hood with its constant barrage. Windshield looks out on a funhouse world through water's lens. Henry sits. He waits, staring at his house. He looks to where a window is lit daytime bright behind curtains. He thinks, did I turn the lights out before I left? He thinks, could I have just forgot? He goes on staring, thinking, wondering if what looks like shadows moving in the house are only a trick of the rain.

The lunchtime crowd has traded their beers for harder tastes. Men in suits from the paper or downtown. Men in coveralls on their way to the mill or just getting back. They sip their spirits from chilled glasses over plates of burgers, of fries dobbed in fat spills of ketchup.

Henry enters the room's chatter and its clink of cutlery, ice dancing in glasses. Meat hissing away. At the counter he lays the briefcase flat.

"Jude."

"Henry."

"Is he still sleeping?"

"Sleeping? He left right after you did."

"But he was out all night."

"Told you not to wake him up."

A moment goes by. One hand plays at the case's strap.

"Did he say where he was going?"

"He tells me nothing. Said he remembered a card game."

"Cards."

"That's about the long and short of it."

Fumbling with the strap now, sliding one loose and then another.

"Do you have a pencil?"

Pulling a bill from within and straightening it on the bar.

"I'm gonna leave a note."

She pulls a stub of pencil from an apron pocket and sets it alongside the bill. She looks at it and she looks at Henry. He takes it up, he jots words in a neat hand. Her eyes on him, narrowed. When he's done he folds it in half and pushes it to her.

"Jude, this is important."

Then he is taking the case in hand, he is turning away. Only when he is gone does she pick up the bill. She unfolds it and reads what is there and folds it again. She puts it and the pencil into the same apron pocket.

"Where'd that fool ever get a hunnered dollar bank note from," asks some lunchtime drunk.

———

The wooden hall is lit but dimly. Like navigating a cave of old. Cliff rounds a corner and another and there sits a man in a simple chair. The man looks up from under the brim of a bent hat and he nods.

"Are they playing?"

The seated man says they are. He gestures at the door. Cliff goes on in.

Men sit around a table. Cards, drinks. The men nod and Cliff nods and he says well. He says a friend asked me to come by as a favor. The men shift in their seats. Some look up, some do not.

"What kind of favor does coming by make?"

"Well. He found some money. He wanted to know if maybe you guys know somebody who lost it."

One man snorts. Another clears his throat.

"Wouldn't you know it, Clifton, but I just was telling the boys how I come to lose some money this very day."

A snicker from the table.

"Funny enough, I too have had a few bucks go missing."

They start to laugh, and another is saying it, and they're all joining in, laughing and confessing their losses and woes.

"Yeah, okay. Okay. I figured as much, but the guy's a sweetheart of a man and I had to ask."

And.

"Is there room to deal me in?"

The sign is lit up with its neon buzz. The day drunks have gone off to dinner or to home. Now men lean across tables talking in whispers or they drink dark liquors and they do not talk at all. Mother Judie sits on a stool behind the counter. In one hand she holds a clear jar. She takes a sip. An old man steps close and orders a drink, and she pours and she takes his money, but she does not move from this spot. She watches the door and she is watching it still when Cliff comes stumbling in. She takes a sip from the jar. He falls into a seat at the counter. His eyelids drift their way closed.

"Where you been all day?"

Eyes shoot open. He stares a moment. He clears his throat.

"Chasing down something for Henry."

"Is that so?"

"Yes ma'am."

She takes a sip.

"Are you gonna tell me or am I gonna have to ask?"

He leans forward and then back again. His lips move in a wordless whisper and he clears his throat again.

"Do what?"

"Arthur Clifton Bent, what kind of trouble are you and that boy into?"

Men at tables have ceased their brooding to watch.

"No trouble. None."

"None."

"I swear."

She takes another sip from her jar and sets it down hard. Liquid sloshes onto fingers, onto the counter. She wipes the hand on her apron and with that hand she takes the hundred dollar note from her pocket and lays it flat on the counter.

"Explain this to me."

He leans down, he slides the bill close. Eyes squint near to shut. He goes on staring at the words written there for some time. When he speaks he says wait. He says, why would he go to a motel?

———

Rain comes now in biblical torrents. It runs along the gutters like miniature rivers. The awning provides an oasis. Cliff steps under its shelter and holds. He brushes loose water from his shoulders and arms but this does nothing. Water pools where he stands.

The door swings wide as he pushes through. A motel clerk stands behind a counter. When he looks up his eyes disappear behind a glare that consumes his glasses' round lenses. He looks down again. Cliff speaks.

"Evening."

The motel clerk nods.

"I'm here looking for my friend."

"Are you now."

Cliff gives the clerk Henry's name. He stands dripping on the carpet. The clerk sets aside a newspaper and turns a page in a ledger. He licks a finger and turns another.

"Oh yes."

He looks up and those eyes again vanish behind fire. He speaks a room number.

"Thank you," says Cliff. The clerk puts a finger to his temple and arcs it in mock salute.

My Lucky Day

Cliff hurries along sidewalk. Each footfall brings a splash. He counts room numbers until he comes to the one sought. Rain falls at his back. It drips down, it runs in his eyes. He wipes at it with the back of a hand. He leans close to the door but there is only quiet. He leans away again. He stares at the closed door. In time he knocks. He waits but no one comes. He knocks again and it is the same. When he touches the knob minutes have passed.

"Henry?"

The door groans inward onto black. He steps inside and now he is gone too.

"Henry?"

He touches the wall and feels for a light switch but there is nothing. He steps forward, and again. His thigh hits the bed. He leans, he pats. Hand touches wood. Bedside table. Lamp. He pulls a chain and there comes a pop and soft light spreads across the room.

The briefcase is there on the floor beside the bed. Cliff turns to stand above it. The straps are undone but the mouth stands closed. The rest of the room is untouched. Bed made and tucked. As if no one has been here.

Cliff takes the folded hundred from a pocket. He lays it on the table under the fall of the lamp's light. With both hands he stretches the bill flat. He stands looking at it there. Time goes by. Then he is leaning again, he is squeezing the lamp's chain. He gives it a gentle pull. The world again is darkness.

ODDS OF LIFE

It hits like a beach ball, landing and bouncing for what must be miles. And it is a beach ball, a million tiny beach balls, layer upon layer of high tech bubble wrap. In time this covering deflates and in its surface a tear appears and through this emerges a mechanical gadget rolling on thick rubber treads.

The rover.

This pilgrim wanders from its now collapsed vessel. Gray sands extend forever. In the distance a colorless mountain. The rover turns in place, its motors whirring. Sensors lick the air. It rolls along, leaving tracks in fine grit. A drill bores holes in ground. It rolls along, it drills down again.

An array of antennae extend and data is hurled into the ether. The call is returned, the voice of home responds, the antennae retract. The rover rolls along, it drills down again.

Time goes on. The rover descends into craters. It climbs hills and dunes. It tastes dirt and sifts through primordial rock. It calls into the ether. The call is returned, the voice of home responds.

In time these quests grow redundant. Each examined wonder has been seen a dozen times, a hundred times, a thousand. Each element tested brings a result long known and stale. This is dirt. This is dirt. This is dirt. Antennae extend, the call goes out. The rover sits. It waits. It sends the call again. It waits. The call is not returned. The voice of home is silent. The rover waits. It sends the call again.

Dust drifts on cold wind. A mound accumulates about the stilled rover. An alien sun passes by, indifferent to the rover's longing. Over and over that star goes on spinning by in the passing of eons. The rover has ceased its calling. The rover has ceased its everything.

Then one day.

Fire cuts the sky. A boiling streak rushes by overhead and in a bright flash disappears in the distance. The rover stirs. It shakes the collected dust of years from its skin. It rolls along.

Land goes by, and days. Then comes a glint still some miles off, a shimmer of some object moving under the touch of that foreign starshine. The rover stops. It sits, waiting, watching. That object moves about, too far off to be discerned, only the periodic flash of sun's reflection making its presence known at all. The rover rolls along.

Features reveal themselves as distance is overcome. A square body is propelled along by eight steel legs.

The crawler.

It bends and leans and a rod probes the soil underneath its form. It turns in place and again tastes the earth. It goes about these tasks on knifeblade legs with arachnic grace.

The rover approaches. The crawler ceases its probing. It raises up, tall and aware. The rover comes near. They each wait. Then, in time, these travelers so far from home extend their sensors, each reaching out for the other.

THE TOWN'S NEW CHURCH

The flock had dwindled for ages. The old going forth to their eternal reward, the young pulled away by the gravity of congealing cityscapes in their orbits. Long before the megachurch went up out by the highway the faithful had begun to move on to take their grace elsewhere.

Pastor Miller was no drunkard. He bore sin, as any man does, but when his sermons began to waver with slur and deep pause those who'd remained of his congregants took note. That first Sunday they whispered. The next they gasped. Each Sabbath following they grew fewer and fewer until the day the pews were empty but for one man.

Roger Tipple was a believer in something. He knew not what, but something. More. He came not of a faith but to be in the presence of whatever he felt in that room. The trickling away of the rows of the long baptized meant little to him, their reason for coming at all was tangential to his own.

Left alone he still listened, awed by Pastor Miller even as the slur deepened, even as the man's vacant eyes stared longer into nothing.

When came the day that he sat in the wooden church hall, quiet without Pastor Miller's teachings, still he stayed and he did smile, basking in the presence of what spirits walked in this sacred place.

He came the next Sunday, and again he was the sole devotee, and him with no pastor, and then once again the Sunday next, but on the fourth Sunday Miller had returned.

"It's great to see you, Pastor."

"And you," he said, clear as day.

The slur had gone. So too had the pause and that empty gaze. The man was there, more than there, more maybe than even before.

"You're looking well."

"A flu got me for a bit, but I'm feeling brand new."

When he took to the pulpit he spoke of redemption and salvation in a manner altered from past sermons. He referenced pacts and deeds done. He looked to the ceiling and the vastness above when he spoke. And then he was done.

Roger Tipple shook the pastor's hand, but the altered way about the man stayed with him. The voice, the cadence. Even the handshake was changed.

The next Sunday brought back only a few, and a few more the Sunday after. The curious hoping for spectacle.

His sermons moved away from tradition. He spoke of whispering statues forgotten long ago in the cracks between mountains. He talked of a door in a room in the desert. He said there was a man who sat in a room looking into a mirror and the face he saw there described abominations he would one day erect. He spoke and they leaned in. He preached of these arcane histories and they found their way back. The flock. In their ones and twos they would repopulate the seats in the little church hall. When he talked they all sighed. At times they cheered.

Roger came to Pastor Miller, and he shook the man's hand, and he asked of these things.

"These are not gospels. Where did these stories come from?""There are gospels in older books," said the pastor. "There are saints whose names time's washed away."

Roger came each Sunday still, and more were there, more were there. He came and he listened. The pastor spoke of sheets of vast dark above. He spoke of ears who would hear a man's prayer when no other would.

When Roger Tipple left he had not felt the presence he'd basked in in that place, not for some time. But the sermons, they go on, and each Sunday more come, each Sunday more come.

CUSTODY OF A RELIC

    Everything is still. The room rests in much the same quiet in which it has waited for decades. Then the deep thunk of a bolt thrown breaks the stillness and a moment later the sound comes again. White dayshine intrudes, and in its fall roused grains do dance like the earth loam in a forgotten tomb touched by air for the first time in millennia.
    The bank is a ruin. The room into which the contractor steps is stopped in time, unchanged and untouched in the years since its surrender to the wash of onrushing past. He moves between desks left much as they had been when the last body sat close, writing up tickets or clearing accounts of patrons in another life. He walks among relics left just as they were like some ersatz Pompeii. Tellers' registers line a long counter in rows with their trays displayed like so many tongues lolling. He touches a lamp whose cord links to nothing. He rolls a pen in place. Two fingers wipe dust on pants thigh. He moves on.
    Round the tellers' station to a hall of open doors furnished with desks and chairs or boxes or nothing at all and beyond this the steel vault entry stands gaping and dark. He brings up a pen light from among items clipped to a belt. Thumb clicks switch. A pale circle of wall appears through the doorway. The contractor enters the vault.
    Shelves lined with only dust take up two walls. The light sweeps across a third to show hundreds of emptied cubbies where once safe deposit boxes were held. Now their doors

stand open and their stores seized or moved or lost. Light moves in absent browse across rows until it stops. He stares and steps near and goes on staring. A single box stays locked away against the wreckage.

He pokes a finger at the lock. He shakes the framework in which the box is set. A folding knife comes out of a pocket. He slides the blade between the metal door and the frame and works it around and tugs and turns the blade and the door comes open with a pop. The box within is dragged from its place among the past and carried through the darkened hall. Something within clanks with his steps. Back in the lobby where day still spills in through the open street door the contractor stops. He lays the box among the dust and pens and tellers' stations. The lid groans its way open. Inside lies a key of stained copper with jagged teeth at one end and a crest at the other adorned with two letters wrapped in ivy. FT

The contractor stares and he is staring still when footsteps break the quiet. A man in a crisp suit is crossing the ground of this hallowed space. When he reaches the contractor he holds out a hand.

"You the contractor?"

The contractor takes the hand and says yes, he says I am.

"Did you hire me?"

"I'm the broker. I'm just the middleman."

"Well."

The broker waits for more but there is no more. He looks down and the key is there in the open box. He nods.

"A key?"

The contractor hooks a thumb to the hall at his back.

"It was in the vault."

"Locked?""Yeah."

"How many others? Boxes, I mean."

"Just the one."

"What does it open?"

"I just found it."

"Who does it belong to?"

The contractor takes up the key. He lifts it and bounces it in his hand, where it carries a surprising heft. He holds it out so the crest is prominent for the broker to see.

"FT would be my guess."

"FT."

The contractor waits.

"Are there records anywhere?"

"Records. Do you know how many years this place has been closed up?" "Okay. Give it over, let me see if I can run it down."

"Give it over?"

"Yeah. Until everything clears I'm responsible for the property. That," the broker points, "is property."

The contractor shakes his head no.

"You said it yourself. You're the middleman."

"Well," he says, "we're in the middle."

The contractor shakes his head again. He says he needs to make a call, he needs to speak to the building's previous owner. He takes up the key and drops it in a pocket and from that pocket he brings a phone as he crosses the room to the street door. Under noonday sun the world is in its constant motion. A car passes and somewhere a vague trickle of song hums on the air. Across the street in an open courtyard silk black grackles drift earthward like so much ash to settle there.

The broker steps into the light where the contractor scrolls his phone. He shakes a cigarette from a pack and puts flame to its tip, breathes in. Smoke drifts on each word.

"Let's get a drink," he says.

The broker smokes as they walk. He points at faded storefronts and crumbling brick facades. He speaks the names of men who own these structures and he disparages these names. The contractor walks along and he nods and returns with the histories of these places, what shops these rooms housed in some other world. Then they are turning in at a nook between storefronts and they are descending concrete steps to a door propped open with a broom jammed behind the hinge. Within, dim figures move but little and somewhere a familiar pop tune from a decade gone by does play. The contractor and the broker move among these shades to a bar that runs the length of a far wall. The broker holds up two fingers and says a word in a Slavic tongue and the small man behind the bar takes a bottle from an array of glass decanters in all shapes and colors. He pours two inches of clear liquid into two glasses and takes up the dollars laid on the bar by the broker.

They sit; the contractor, the broker. They slide onto barstools and sip for some time. Neither man speaks. Then.

"It's a technicality, is what it is."

The broker. The contractor sips and he nods.

"I'd agree with that."

"We'll never find who it belonged to."

"Okay."

"Here it's in limbo."

The contractor sips and says nothing.

"It's probably worthless."

"Well. I don't agree with that."

"What does that mean?"

"It could open anything. It was in that box for a reason."

The broker empties his glass in a gulp and orders another and with the glass sweating onto the fingers holding it he sits in quiet for the span of a minute. When he speaks he says technically it's not yours, and technically it's not mine, and no one else knows it exists. So.

"We could sell it."

The contractor turns and stares.

"It's a key."

"Yes."

"To God knows what."

"Yes."

"Who are we going to sell it to?"

"I have an idea."

"You have an idea."

The broker nods.

"Do you know the auctioneer?"

———

It was a barn once. Blue, not the red of tradition. The broker knocks at a door warped and faded and a voice somewhere on the other side hollers come in and the two men do just that. An office. A man seated behind a desk watches them come.

"Boys."

The broker says hello and he introduces the contractor and the contractor nods.

The man behind the desk takes a straw panama from his head and sets it on the desk among a jumble of boxes and miscellany. The broker says this man runs the auction house. Hands are shaken all around. The auctioneer's face is damp with sweat and splotched in places with red and he is visibly drunk.

"You buying or selling?"

"Well," says the broker, "we've got a trinket we're not sure what to do about."

The auctioneer looks at the two men. He leans to the desk and runs a hand over hair white and thin. The hand comes away wet.

"What kind of trinket are we dealing with?"

The broker waves a hand at the contractor and the contractor takes the key from his pocket. He places it on the desk with a dense thunk. The auctioneer pushes spectacles up on his nose and he leans over the key and stares. He does not pick it up, he does not touch it. The broker pulls over a chair and sits. The contractor remains on his feet. There is quiet for some time.

Then.

"Well I won't auction that. What are you asking for it?"

The contractor looks at the broker. The broker gives a meager shrug.

"What's it worth?"

The auctioneer speaks without taking his gaze from where the key lies.

"It costs what you buy it for."

"What does that mean?"

"It means it's worth whatever somebody agrees to pay for it. As much or as little."

"Well. How much or how little are you willing to pay?"

Now the auctioneer does look up. For long seconds he stares hard at the broker.

"Where did you get this?"

The broker grips chair sides and shifts his weight, hauls himself up in his seat. He turns to the contractor and then back to the auctioneer.

"It was in the old bank building. In the vault."

"Do you know what it opens?"

Broker: "I don't even know who it belongs to."

Contractor: "The files are all decades gone. All the boxes were supposed to have been shipped off to wherever way back when."

The auctioneer sits with this. He goes on staring. In time he takes up the key and holds it flat in his palm, lifting its weight and lowering it again, two times, three.

"I'll give you five hundred."

"Five?"

The auctioneer nods.

"How'd you get there?"

"Well what do you want for it?"

"Not five," says the broker.

"Why?" "It's an antique."

"It's a novelty."

"It's potential. It could open anything. Auction that off. Potential."

The auctioneer takes off his glasses and folds the arms with care. He slides them into a jacket pocket.

"How about this?"

He reaches into an assortment of packages stacked alongside the desk and sorts until he comes to a box carved in oiled wood. He sweeps aside items on the desk and sets the box among the cleared space.

"What about a trade?"

He pulls a latch and there comes a click and he lifts the lid.

"Antiques. Came in this week."

Set in purple velvet, each facing opposite the other, lies two dueling pistols etched in intricate design with creatures of lore, mermaids in vivid detail reaching out for some figure unseen and forgotten.

The broker: "Guns."

The auctioneer: "A dueler's friend. The violence of a righteous man."

The contractor watches the auctioneer. The broker leans over the desk.

"What're they worth?"

"More than five hundred."

"But how much?"

"It costs what you buy it for."

The broker leans back. He sits in silence a moment. Then.

"Then why trade?"

"I don't exactly have a license for these at the moment. They'll sit on a shelf for months. As that, they're a bauble I can't sell. You have a novelty I can."

The broker eyes the auctioneer as if he expects something else to come but the auctioneer lets the quiet play out.

"That's it?" says the broker.

"Near enough."

The contractor steps to the desk and takes up the key. Only after it is slipped into a pocket does he speak up.

"We'll give it some thought."

The broker looks up at the contractor. The auctioneer puts a hand on his hat where it lay.

"Well," he says.

The lunch drinkers have gone and the ones who will come with dark are still some hours off. A handful of forms lift drinks and order drinks and speak but little. A horse race plays on more than one television.

"I'm gonna go with, it's a case of finders keepers."

The contractor says it with a nod. He throws back a shot of golden drink and he gulps. The broker shakes his head and takes a hard pull from a glass of some clear thing poured high. A bartender hovers, not quite nearby and not quite not. A small man but not the same one as before. The contractor orders another shot and the bartender comes close and pours and retreats, and when he is gone the contractor speaks.

"We could flip for it."
"We're not gonna do that."
"Fight you for it."
"Not that either."

Time loses its footing in quiet and drink and the white noise of steady bar hum. When some time later the broker speaks he says what if there's a way. A way to find the owner, come to think of it.

"We could maybe get a reward, split it, be washed of the thing."

The contractor sets down a half done shot he's been holding for some minutes. He turns. When he speaks he does so with one eye closed.

"You got an idea?"
"I do."

―――

The library sign says CLOSED but the lights on the other side of the windows are all still lit. The broker knocks on the glass while the contractor leans on a railing running alongside the front walk. A woman appears in the foyer, thirty-something, floral dress. She points at the sign and she waits. The broker knocks again.

"Is the old man here?"

She squints, she sighs. She steps close to the door but does not throw the bolt that holds it fast.

"He's out for a walk."
"That old man can barely stand."

She gives a deep shrug. The two men only wait. She speaks.

"Give it a half hour or so. You can come in when he's here."

"We'll be back."

He knocks on the glass once more but she has already turned away.

———

Bottles line shelves in every direction, tinctures of colored glass in all manner of shape and size. The contractor takes one down and the broker takes down another and the contractor puts the first back. They wander, they browse. In time they migrate to a long counter lined with smaller versions of the bottles populating the rows of shelves. The clerk says a number and the broker lays down a card. The clerk runs the card and the machine beeps and the clerk says it's uh it says no. The second card he tries goes through and none among them comment on the scene.

When the two men leave they carry the bottle in a paper bag marked with no logo or print. They talk but little as they walk and each man sips from the bottle more than once. When they come to once more stand at the library door the last of the day's sun has come close to finishing its falling away. The woman again appears at the broker's knock and she holds up a finger and disappears into the room beyond. When she returns she holds a card that she swipes alongside an inner door that now stands closed. She opens this and in the foyer throws a bolt and pushes open the front entrance.

"Don't keep him long. I'm finishing up and taking him home."

The contractor nods, the broker says sure thing.

The two men follow the librarian through a wide span of room arranged in a maze of old tomes and beyond this hallways carpeted in a thick cloth that seems to swallow up every fraction of sound. She stops at a door and opens it but does not go in.

"A few minutes."

The broker nods. "Just a few minutes."

And.

"Yeah," says the contractor.

The two men step into a square cubby of a room furnished with a simple table and two chairs. A man draped in ancient flesh sits turning the yellowed pages in a book of old maps. He looks up at their presence and adjusts glasses with lenses an inch thick and looks down again. The two men step to the table. They wait for some moment that doesn't come and after their wait the contractor lays the key on the table. The old man's gaze shifts to where the key lay and then back to his book.

After some seconds.

"Mmhmm."

The broker speaks.

"Can you tell me what this is?"

The old man leans forward. He adjusts his glasses and looks over the object and he leans away again.

"That's a key."

"I mean. Do you have any idea who it belongs to?"

The old man folds a page in the book. He closes it shut and leans back, crossing one leg over the other.

"John, this is not my job anymore."

"I'd appreciate it."

"Well hell then."

"There could be a reward."

"There isn't."

"How would you know that?"

The old man sighs. He takes a bent pack of cigarettes from a shirt pocket and lights it with a metal lighter dotted in rust.

"Dad, you can't smoke in here."

The voice comes from somewhere beyond the open door.

"I been smokin in here a hunnert year."

"It's a law, dad."

He says nothing. After a throw of moments she appears in the doorway.

"Open the window, at least."

She pulls shut the door and is gone. The old man inhales on the cigarette. He opens his mouth and lets smoke roll in that maw. He points a gnarled hand at the paper bag the broker holds and he waves it his way. The broker passes it over. The old man unscrews the top and drinks deeply and gasps. He wipes his wet mouth and passes the bottle back across the table. With the same hand he gestures at the key.

"Where'd you turn that up?"

"The old bank. It was in the vault."

"In the vault?"

The broker: "In a box."

The contractor: "The only box there was."

The old man nods. He breathes in smoke.

"Uh huh. The only box there was."

Then he is quiet, leaning back, slumped in his chair as he stares at the key where it lay.

"You know what it is?" "We been through that."

"But you know what it opens?"

"Don't know that."

"You know who it belongs to."

"I know who it did."

"Who's that?"

"Man name of Francis."

"How do you know?"

The old man leans over the table to tap with the cigarette hand at the FT at the key's top.

"Crest."

"A crest."

"Mmhmm."

"Does he have people?"

The old man looks off at nothing, and after a moment he shakes his head.

"None I know of."

"No one who might know what this goes to. No one who might want it."

The old man smokes and says well, he says someone might. Some museum, collector. If you find the right one.

"Who was this guy?"

The old man gives a deep shrug.

"Before my time."

Acres of manicured grasses colored in an unreal green are surrounded by aluminum benches stacked and rowed in mock coliseum. The town's high school name is stenciled on a hundred surfaces that show purple and white under two pale floodlights, one across the field from the other, and in the field's middle sits the contractor and the broker where the shadows run deepest. They talk of possession and ownership and value. The contractor drinks and he passes the bag and the broker drinks. They talk of the righteousness of ownership and the reality of possession. They pass the bag and they drink. The lights pop off one and then the other and the two men drink. They talk of potential. The talk slows and then it falls into the long, empty quiet of night.

The world is the soft bruise of near morning. Grass stands damp with fresh dew. The two men stir and groan and in slow fashion come awake still fogged in a drunk. The broker asks a question and clears throat and does not receive an answer. The contractor wipes his face and unscrews the bottle top and drinks. Somewhere a whistle blows and voices speak or shout, but not here, not in this place. The broker takes a drink. He looks at the contractor.

"I have an idea."

He says it like it's a joke, and maybe it is and maybe it isn't.

"We could duel for it."

The bag is passed between the two men and the talk becomes a kind of dare and the sun comes closer to day. Then the bottle is empty and the bag is left in the grass as the contractor and the broker cross the field and exit through an open gate. Beyond this there lies a gravel lot and then a wire fence surrounding a wide pasture peopled by hovering cows who look up and blink at the passing of these two wraiths before going back to grinding cud in their dumb jaws or huffing steam into day's first light. Beyond this is a blue barn.

The contractor stands at a window. He says are you sure and the broker says yes, he says it like it's maybe a joke or maybe a dare, and the contractor puts out the glass with a rock. He climbs over the sill and a minute later he is climbing black out with a box carved in oiled wood. He pulls a latch and there comes a click. He lifts the lid and removes two antique pistols with mermaids carved into the old wood. He takes out powder and ball and he tosses away that box with its lined velvet of purple. He looks at the broker and the broker nods and he loads and arms one pistol and then the other. He hands one to the broker. He says okay.

"Okay," says the broker back. He says it like it's a joke and then he walks some dozen paces into grassland. The contractor follows along in something of a stumble. The broker is smiling.

"Then we let fate decide who is a righteous man."

He says it like it's a joke, and the two men step away from each other, and they turn and raise their pistols, but neither of these duelers is a righteous man.

HEMINGWAY

The Hemingway I met was in 1959 on the southern beaches of some foreign locale. He would sit in the window of a house that didn't belong to him and all day long he would drink from a cheap glass and smile at pretty girls in frilly bathing suits. Sometimes they would mouth something sarcastic and he would laugh like he didn't understand and somehow the joke was always on them.

I knew nothing of the man's works and I knew nothing of his life. He was a name I had heard and a personality I enjoyed. He took me to parties and he laughed and he drank and he was the most interesting man I had ever met. People looked at him even as he was doing nothing and the town was always at the table.

It's days or more later and I'm alone at a café when a face I've seen around several times but still the face of a stranger takes me aside and speaks to me in hushed tones. I shrug off his words and I shrug off those of the next man to say them, but it isn't long before I can't shrug them off anymore.

People would say to me he's a liar.

"Hemingway is a liar?"

They would say he's a cheat and a thief.

"Hemingway is a cheat? Hemingway is a thief?"

No. You're not getting it.

"He is not Ernest Hemingway. That man is a bad man."

It's a party like any of the dozen others, the hundred others I've found myself in on this island of turmoil and beauty. Hemingway is laughing and he is telling stories that don't belong to him. He is looking at me and he is raising a glass.

"To life."

I put my hand on his shoulder and I squeeze like an old friend. I smile into the bearded face of a man I don't know. I put my knife in his ribs. I push and I feel cloth tear and flesh tear and something else underneath. His eyes grow wide and they grow distant.

And I wonder, will the real Hemingway's eyes grow wide when I stab him? Will they grow distant?

THE LATEST MODEL

A cheap printed sign reads ANTIQUES, ELECTRONICS, ODDITIES. Another says OPEN in neon blue hum. Each window is caged in twined wire mesh. Behind it lies a room cluttered with rows of assorted miscellany and each open space bathed in feeble yellow glow.

A man enters the shop under a bing bong of artificial chime and the jaundiced illumination washes across his being. The insistent dim obscures his features such that in catching a glimpse of his own image in a series of mirrors leaned against one wall they each contain the face of a stranger.

A counter divides the room. A display case packed with shelves of no one thing. Guns, watches, rings, arranged as if scattered with a toss. Nothing is labeled, nothing is priced. The front of the case is lined with the same chicken cage as the shop's front. Large padlocks hang.

The proprietor smiles. He stands leaning against this display of collected wares. The proprietor is a small man, a square one. He wears an old suit coat sewn from a cloth thick and checkered. Time has worn stitching loose in places. His hair is the color of straw. It is thin and stands in strings combed away from his face. He is speaking before the customer is at the counter.

"We've got what it is you're after."

"I don't know what I'm after."

"Even better."

"I need a gift."

"Wife? Mom?"

"My brother's birthday."

"We've got that."

"I don't know."

"Take a look, you'll find it, but even if you don't, narrow your search, give me a few days and I'll turn it up."

The proprietor pulls a card from a tray of them and slides it in front of the customer. It reads CONSTANCE SALT and SALES. A phone number is printed at the bottom.

"What kind of name is that?"

"An old one."

The customer again looks at the card. He puts it away in a pocket. The proprietor watches. He goes on smiling.

"Tell me about the brother."

"What about him?"

"What does he like?"

"He likes gadgets. Electronics. I saw your sign."

The proprietor nods.

"He used to collect old video games."

"What does he collect now?"

"Not those. They took up the whole garage. Racks floor to ceiling. His wife made him clean house."

"What now?"

"Radios. TVs. Sometimes he gets them and they're all beat to hell, but he keeps the nameplates, you know? The brand label."

"A real connoisseur then."

"He would say so."

The proprietor taps his fingers on his thumb, one, two, three, four. He makes a noise like a word, hmmm. He pulls a ring of keys from his belt where it connects to an expanding length of chain.

"I have just the thing."

He puts the key into a lock set in the countertop and turns it and lifts a bridge section back to open a walkway into the shop's other half. He waves the customer on and the customer steps through and he shuts and locks the section back in place.

"We keep the exotics back here, away from the riffraff."

He pulls the same ring of keys and sorts until he finds one in particular and he opens a cabinet, and he sorts again and he opens another, and a third. He unsnaps a padlock and opens a gate made from still more chicken wire.

"What do you think?"

"They're TVs."

"And radios."

"They're nice."

"Each piece is unique."

"I don't know which ones he has."

"Friend, he doesn't have any of these."

"He's got a good collection."

"Not these. Turn it on."

"Which one?"

"Any one."

Shelves are lined with contraptions. Housings of oiled wood with tweed patched speakers. Cabinets inside cabinets. Dials and knobs and tubes. All manner of size and configuration. The customer makes a choice and he turns a knob on a boxy wooden piece and a song begins to play.

"What is that?""Duke Ellington."

"No, I mean like a tape deck?"

"Nope."

"Is it an MP3?"

"It is not."

And.

"Try another."

A smaller one now, plastic and teal. Static and then song.

"Is that Frankie Valli?"

"There you go."

Another, arched and gothic. The proprietor smiles.

"Ah, Cole Porter. I love Cole Porter."

"What is this?"

"It's the radio."

"But what's the trick? Nobody's playing these songs."

"These are antiques. They're set in their ways. Do you want to try a TV?"

The customer's eyes widen.

"No I do not."

The proprietor shrugs. He turns the radio off.

"If I buy one will you tell me?"

"Jesus. If it rains do you ask the clouds how they got there? It's a radio. It plays what it knows. Now are you buying or are we gonna keep flirting?"

"What's that?"

He points to a square of gray metal. The tubes and dials are gone, the little orange diodes are all stripped away. It has a single button on its top.

"That's the latest model."

The proprietor presses the button. He looks from the gray box to the customer's face. He waits. The customer looks only at the box. The absence of sound is more than silence. It is a profound void where the background hum of being should be. He hears the void. He knows this silence.

"Turn it off."

The proprietor smiles. He presses the button again. The presence of that silence vanishes.

"I don't understand."

"You will," says the proprietor. "But not today. This item is not for sale."

The customer laughs and the proprietor stares and the customer stops. He grows quiet. The proprietor speaks.

"So. What'll it be?"

"Can I think about it? Come back tomorrow?"

The proprietor's eyes narrow. His nostrils flare and then contract.

"You can do anything you want, friend."

He moves close and then past the customer and he raises the counter's gate and waits. The customer returns to the other side of the counter. He turns, and the proprietor is shutting cabinets, and he is snapping padlocks closed. He sees the customer watching and offers a mock salute. The customer steps into the night.

The street is damp with a rain that has only just ended or is about to start. The customer stands. He touches the card in his pocket. The lettering. He drops it in the gutter, where it drifts along and disappears into a storm drain. The neon blue of the open sign blinks out, and some moments later Cole Porter begins to play.

THOMAS IS A LIAR

Thomas is a liar. When Thomas was twelve, Thomas ate all the candy in the candy jar. When his mother asked who ate all the candy, Thomas said that a monster ate it, because Thomas is a liar.

When Thomas was in high school, Thomas cut class. When the principal asked Thomas where he'd been, Thomas said he'd been in class the whole time, because Thomas is a liar.

When Thomas got the new car, Thomas ran over a man in the road. When the man died in his arms, Thomas said he was sorry, because Thomas is a liar.

When Thomas was being led to the gas chamber, Thomas seemed confused. When the guard asked Thomas if he knew why he was here, Thomas said no, because Thomas is a liar.

But Thomas didn't really go to the gas chamber. Thomas didn't really run over the man in the road. Thomas didn't really cut class or eat all the candy. Thomas didn't do any of these things, because Thomas is a liar.

WRONG NUMBER

    First comes the knock. Unhurried tapping from the door's other side. Frederic rises and he pulls open the door and the hall is empty of life. He turns each way as if something might change but it does not. He crosses the hall and he knocks himself and the neighbor answers. A small man with no hair and a week's beard.
    "Did you just come to my door?"
    "Is that a riddle?"
    "What?"
    "You're at my door. No, I did not come to yours."
    A bell begins to ring. A phone. Frederic takes it from his pocket. The name on the screen reads PATRICIA. He presses a button.
    "Hello?"
    "Hello?" A woman's voice. "Hello?"
    A click and then nothing.
    "Who was that?"
    "I don't know?"
    "What was the number?" "It said Patricia."
    "Who is Patricia?"
    "I don't know."

    He wakes under blankets pulled to his neck. Sheets damp with sweat. He doesn't remember the dream. The bell is chiming and he does not know at first that this is what woke him but it is. He takes up the phone, he presses a button, but there is no one there.

The window is open. Birds sing their nightsong and the night hums of invisible things. Crickets, cicadas. He puts his feet on the floor. He turns the phone in his hand but the screen is dark and he tells himself this was the dream.

He is late. He checks the clock, he's overslept. He dials his brother but there is no answer. He tries again and again no one is there.

He enters the garage to echoes. He is alone in this place. The middle of the day. The cars of night workers populate the space but sparsely. A long square of car built by young men now old drips oil into a spreading pool like the vestiges of some arterial calamity. Frederic gets in. He turns a key and he utters profane words and he turns the key again. He gets out.

He walks for a block, and another, and another. Loose road crunches under each step. Somewhere in the distance highway traffic huffs in its constant passing. He tries to call his brother. Nothing. He lowers the phone. Its bell begins to chime. The screen says PATRICIA. The bell quiets. He presses the name and a number appears. He reads it aloud. He closes his eyes and says the number again. When he opens his eyes the screen is blank. He repeats the number as he dials. A tone plays, not a ringing but something flat, and then a click and then nothing. He looks at the phone. The screen is black. He presses a button and it doesn't light up. He shakes it. He puts it back in his pocket.

A car pulls alongside. Silver and sleek and rounded. A window comes down.

"Freddy, what are you doing?"

"I'm supposed to pick up Mike."
"I mean why are you walking?"
"Car's dead as hell, Rob."
"What's wrong with it?"
"It won't start."
And.
"Do you know where there's a payphone?"
"Sure, Fred. Up ahead, go right, then keep going till you hit 1987."
"That's helpful, Robert."
"Come on, let me take you up to Mike's. Use his phone, then we'll see about getting him wherever he's going."
And. "What's wrong with your phone?"
"It's dead."

―――

The office is a wash of air conditioning and faded blue carpet. Someone in a room somewhere talks on a phone but their words are noise, eroded by the AC's churn. Robert disappears around a corner. Frederic turns down a hall and knocks on a door and enters.

A man sits at a desk. Thin and tall and dark hair uncombed. Mike.

"Where have you been?"
"Robert's gonna give you a ride."
"Robert."

Frederic points to the hall at his back. Mike looks that way. Frederic speaks.

"My phone died. Can I use your computer for a minute?"

Mike waves a hand at his desk as he leaves the room.

The first search is just the word Patricia with the name of the town. He scrolls and he reads and it's nothing. He searches the number and the hits are all old, the line is defunct. More info costs money. He takes a card from a tray inside the desk. He gets an address, he gets a map. This he prints out, but when he sees the street name he already knows what is there.

Voices in the hall. Robert, Mike. They talk in words lost in the din. Frederic folds the printout and puts it in a pocket. He steps into the hall.

"Can you drop me off too?"

———

The silver dollop of car pulls to a stop along the dam. Frederic steps out onto the berm. The others are laughing.

"I'll walk back."

He shuts the door. When they are gone he crosses the road and moves down toward the water below. Feet slide on gravel. He steadies and walks and when the ground levels out he sits. He is five feet from the lake.

A boat moves in the distance, circling and moving off and returning again. He takes the paper from his pocket. The map of this lost place. He wads the paper and tosses it but it falls shy of the water and rolls and sits. Wet rocks soaking, the crumple coming undone. A kind of melting.

The boat circles back, and now he can hear them, young people laughing, whooping, and then they are turning once more, fading and soon gone. Long after they've vanished in the distance the ripples of their wake rise and fold in on themselves and continue a dance beyond any temporal translation by the compartmented observer, and as their crests fade and become lost in the infinite sway, Frederic begins to weep.

TWO INCHES OF TAPE

The little strip of black electrical tape stuck to the nicotine-stained wall like a band-aid slapped in the middle of a plaster desert. One corner hung loose, the glue just starting to let go, giving in to age.

The tape was the only piece of furniture in the room.

The new tenant was no one important. A lot like the old tenant. He moved into Apartment C with almost nothing. A paper sack filled with food, a duffle bag filled with everything else.

The new tenant had no furniture to fill the room.

He noticed the little strip of black electrical tape the first time he was there, the day the landlord showed him the apartment. He asked about it, idle curiosity and that alone.

"Oh, that," said the landlord.

It was still there when the new tenant moved in with his past and his future shoved into two uninspiring bags. A nook that passed for a kitchen, a closet that looked like a bathroom, sink and toilet and hot plate and a few feet of floor. And that little strip of tape. Home.

He didn't touch it at first, this new tenant. He set his things in a corner and closed the door. He tapped the antique thermostat. He ran a shoe over a stain on the carpet. These are the things he did before he decided he had to know.

The little strip of black tape came up with a single quick tug. Warm glue stuck to the new tenant's fingers. He wiped it on his sleeve but it persisted. The tape he tossed at his feet.

A small black spot showed where the tape covered a moment before. A hole the size of a dime. Paint chipped at the hole's edges, small fissures running out in uncaring directions.

It was no time at all before the new tenant began to pick at these.

The chips came off like broken scabs, a few at first and then more and faster. Flakes fell to the floor of the little apartment with its dirty floor and featureless existence, a dust of pieces landing on the toes of the new tenant's shoes. The more he picked at the cracks, the wider the hole became. Soon the little hole became a big hole.

Soon it became much more than that.

The new tenant picked at his wall day and night. Wall became walls and still he could not stop. Flakes became strips and on he went. The new tenant wept when his fingers began to leave long bloody smears on the pieces of wall he tore away but this he did not feel, those tears not real or at least not his own.

Days or weeks or something more went by without notice. Nothing existed but the new tenant and the hole he'd created. The hole he'd found. He tore and he ripped and he peeled away the world around him until one day he looked at the place there had once been walls, had once been an ugly little apartment, a floor and a bathroom and what might pass for a kitchen. He looked at the place he thought he would learn to call home but all that remained was a wide black hole running forever in all directions.

SOME TROUBLE NEXT DOOR

The dogs won't stop. They're barking, they're yipping. The sound of their bodies hitting the fence with some force comes and comes again.

Andrew turns the blinds but he sees only streetlight falling onto the road. He thinks, maybe I'll go over there. He thinks, shut those dogs up. He twists the blinds closed.

A raised voice comes, its edges softened by walls. It quiets and then it is there again. Not quite a shout and not quite not. Man or woman. A voice determined but vague. The dogs go on barking.

Andrew sits. He thinks, I'll put on a movie, but he does not. He thinks, it's fine, it's fine.

Blue and red swirls flash beyond the window. He stands, he lifts a blind to look out. A patrol car idles at the curb. He waits. Lights go on spinning. He sits down again. The hour weighs. He lets his eyes fall shut. When he opens them the lights are gone.

He starts. He thinks, I've fallen asleep. He sits forward. He touches his face. He thinks there was a noise, he tries to remember. And here it comes again. A gentle knock. Tap, tap, tap at the door.

He lifts a blind, and a man is there. A stranger, fresh-faced, hair combed, eyes ahead at the door. The stranger's face is placid, mouth flat, neutral, an arrangement of features in between expressions.

Andrew taps at the window.

The neutral face at first flinches, it recoils, and then it is animating, it is reworking itself in the approximation of something familiar and safe. A smile, friendly. The stranger points at the door.

"No," says Andrew.

The stranger goes on smiling. He points to the door again. Andrew shakes his head. He again says no. The stranger frowns, he looks puzzled. He turns his eyes to the door. Andrew lets the blinds fall shut. He is backing away, he's looking from window to door and back. He sits down. Minutes go by. Then the sound comes, that tap, tap, tap. He closes his eyes. He holds them closed tight. Heart thumps. He breathes, in, out, in.

The sound has not come again, does not come again. Time has come loose. Five minutes, an hour, he does not know. He thinks, have I been asleep? He thinks, is it over?

When he opens his eyes the lights are there. Red and blue flashing, brighter now. The window is filled up with their insistence. He stands, he comes close. He reaches a hand to the blinds. Those lights go on, they spin and spin and spin. He leans in, he listens. He waits. He swallows with throat dry. He breathes, he waits for some change. The dogs are all silent now.

WHISPER TO TRUMPET

Death was no surprise. Gill had been unwell as long as anyone could remember. Bad lungs. Wheezing, coughing. Drowning. He spoke in a whispered lilt when he did speak; to his friends, to his sister, Jane. His laughter was silent and often.

As a child he liked the song of old lounge crooners, each whiskey-thick tune reaching something inside, a longing for voice he could name but only just. He wanted a sound for himself, something rich or deep or just different, something textured or wild. He wished for it, he prayed.

When Gill was in school and Jane came down dressed for prom her friends all cheered and clapped. Gill clapped along with them, he put his lips together in mock wolf whistle but the sound he made was a huff. They laughed and he reddened and they left but his shame stayed. He prayed for a voice, any other sound. He closed his eyes and wished again and again.

At the end they came to see him; Gill's friends, Jane. His friends told jokes and shared memories and they laughed and he laughed too, silent, often, and when they were gone she sat with him. They talked, her in rich tones and he in his whisper. She asked what can I do and he said oh nothing, nothing. Just.

"I wish I could sing a song," he said. "I wish. I could even just whistle."

She stared and then she laughed and he laughed too, silent and full of joy.

She held his hand when he was gone and long after.
And so.

Some god or other, as they do in their whimsy, having heard these lamentations year after year and in its omnipotence not understanding the weight of their despair, took interest in this faithful case of want, and that is how Whispering Gill came to be reborn as a trumpet.

THE DREAM HOTEL

Every night he enters the hotel. The front door is always open. He moves through a foyer and another door beyond. Here a window running the length of a wall off to the right lets light fall onto a sunken lobby. Couches are all arranged in modern style. Ahead a raised walkway leads to elevators going up or down. To the left is a door.

Each night he heads forward. He goes up to a room or to showcased acts the hotel puts on, old timey numbers done up in a smoke-filled lounge. He enters a library where the leather of old books fills every wall. Sometimes he goes down to empty corridors winding in on themselves for miles. He walks wandering through the night. He does not go to the right, that way there is only a place to sit out the hours in the slow movement of light. The lone door to the left remains untouched.

It all feels real. Sometimes more real than real. He falls into a hotel bed and waits for the dream that's already there to begin. He passes a face he knows from some other life and he nods and it's ordinary, it is not magic and it is not a memory, it is a moment happening only in forever now.

The nights in the hotel, they go on, the same moments packed or repacked, over and over. He's wrapped warm in soft sheets or he passes a smiling face between places. He touches the spines of books he does not open though he can smell the ancient ink on their pages. He wanders a maze of nothing for hours in the stacked catacombs below. Every night is some version of the same. Over and over and over. The same faces, the same rooms. A hundred times. A thousand. Ten thousand. More.

The night does come that he turns to the left toward that one closed door, he doesn't know why, and he does not wonder why through these eons he's not once veered that way. He touches the knob, and it turns, it is not locked. He gives the door a shove.

The black that opens before him consumes, it pulls. He steps closer as if some distant shape might coalesce in even the vaguest outline if only he could step out of the light to better see, but before him stands only infinite black. Still there is a sound. A whisper, a hint of voice. He moves closer and closer still. He hears words spoken somewhere far off in that gloom. He listens to the words as they come.

When he pulls the door shut there comes a soft click. He does not touch the door again.

He enters the hotel and he enters it again, every night, as he has each night for as long as he can remember. The front door is there, it opens for him as always. He goes on, he goes up or down, night after night.

It's the faces he notices first. The smiling passersby in the foyer. Their features sag with loose skin, eyes jaundiced but wide with some deep fury, as if enraged by his seeing. They nod or say hello or just smile. They never, ever blink. The lounge's songs lose their tune, become discordant cries barely held together. The halls down below run with sweat on their walls, patches of dark standing out and dripping to pool on the floor.

Comes the night when he is alone in the hotel. The faces are gone, the songs have all fallen silent. When he goes to the library each book in his hand turns to dust. Cracks riddle the hallways below, deep fissures streaming black waters ankle deep. There is a hum, a tone felt in flesh. A vibration in the air. The lights above flicker.

He still goes. He forever will go. But the lights are all dark now, the shutters pulled low. He tries the handle but the door has no give. The hotel is shut to him on the nights he sleeps at all.

COMES THE SORROWER

It is a totem of some renown. The tree first stood alone in a field, and the people would come, they would make their wishes, they would go. In time they came and they stayed, they built their town, their town where at its heart stands the wishing tree.

It grows at a slant unnatural and enchanting. Just the barest hint of wickedness, this daring to be unique. Still it stands tall and thick, allowed to grow old, older than the town around it, older than the nation.

New people come now. They come to see, they come to wish. When the leaves are a deep green they come from across the map to lean in and whisper quiet desires, some sweet, some dark, or they take a photo, or they kiss the face there.

It's only a knot, the face in the tree. It's only the vaguest sense of a man looking out of that trunk. The stories are gossip passed around since always, since the time before the town was a town. Ghost stories, legends. He was a man of great sin whose Lord had had enough and punished the way gods delight in punishing. Or he was some sort of healer who failed to save the life of a wise man's daughter, and that wise man in his rage did summon all his long life's knowledge to punish the healer for this failure. Or he was just a man who lost a love, and when she was gone he stood weeping atop her grave until his body took root and he was forever trapped alone in his grief.

Comes the sorrower. The wishing tree's leaves have gone the rich red of autumn when the sorrower under dark of night comes, alone in the park with the tree and the man in the tree and her secret wish. With her she brings her sorrow, though to lessen this burden is not the wish she will make, for this sorrow and others are among the great many things that make up her spirit. The sorrower crosses open ground on silent step and she comes to the tree and she leans to the face there and with a bare breath of words she shares her wish. She lets her hands play across the ancient rind and she speaks her wish again. Her weight presses there, and she gasps, and she speaks her wish again. She throws a leg over the trunk, she squeezes the wood with her thighs. She pulls herself forward and back and forward again so that the face is beneath her, touching her. She speaks her wish again. She begins to move her body. She speaks her wish in a whisper and she speaks it in a moan and she grinds herself against that face, and her arms do rise, and her fingers play across her tingling skin, and she speaks her wish, she speaks her wish, and limbs like hands intertwine with her fingers, and she is speaking her wish, she is crying it out.

And now she is spent, she is slumped across the cool flesh of the tree. She lies there panting, her body wrapped around the dark wood. In the sky the moon hangs as it has done, always there through the centuries for the face in the tree to look up and see.

The sorrower leaves this place this night, but when she finds her wish has come true, and it will, and she does, she will come once more to the wishing tree with its cursed man to offer her wish again.

ROMANCE NOVEL

Before

The street lies in dark. A burned-out lamp leaves a hole in the world. At the corner another pole is fitted with a glow of soft yellow. Gentle night sun. Here there is darkness, a swatch cut from the articulation of existence. Windows move with phantom shapes, these pockets of warmth scattered in the void like shadows on a cave wall. All else is black.

John Jeffrey Digby sits in the driveway. Lawn chair dragged and sagging. The garage stands open at his back, light off, as dark as the rest. He puffs a cigar. Smoke rolls and wafts. Highway traffic moves along a mile in the distance. A song plays somewhere, not here. Old. Fifties and saccharine. The one with the lollipop.

"John."

He leans toward her voice.

"What are you doing out here?"

"Go back inside."

"You'll never be mayor talking like that."

"Dad was."

Headlights break the dark. A car advances and rolls to a stop at the curb and there it idles, the grumbling of an old engine's churn. The headlights go out and the car becomes a part of the night.

"Give me some of that."

She reaches for the cigar and he pulls away.
"Angela, go inside."
And.
"Don't smoke in the house."

Then she is turning and she is moving through the dark to the door and in. The hall is lit but dimly. She takes a band from a wiry wrist and ties back hair run through with streaks of gray. She turns again to the door. Waiting.

Then.

Down the hall to the kitchen. She pulls open the refrigerator and reaches behind stacked butters and brings out a bent pack of cigarettes. A cheap plastic lighter, see through and green. She thumbs the strike and nothing. She rubs the strike's metal with warm hands. She shakes a cigarette loose and pulls it free with her lips and she thumbs the strike again and breathes fire. Eyes half-lidded. Slow exhale. A plume blossoms. She takes the cigarette in two fingers and inhales again.

She steps back into the garage. Thought is replaced with nothing. She stands very still, she stares into the black. His chair is a shape in the driveway, now empty. His cigar's bloom of fire is a dying glow in the gutter where it has fallen and rolled. Nothing moves in the street. Night crickets saw and chirp. Somewhere the highway huffs along.

"Johnny?" she says.

1

The pounding insists. It breaks and comes again and now it does not stop.

"I'm here, I'm here, I'm here."

Edward pads along the hall. He touches his face and opens the door and the night is gone. In its place is the spinning blue of police flashers and lights transfixed and day bright. Cars line the street. They stretch around the corner, parked idling in disarray. Men stand among them or they move up the walks to households not yet roused.

A man is at the door. Cop. Square face and eyes a glint in pits of shadow. He takes a step and Edward moves back. He says May I come in but he is already inside. He takes another step. Then he is past and he's moving along the hall, he is leaning in each doorway he finds.

"This your place?"

"My uncle's."

"He around?"

"He travels for work."

The cop stops and turns. He looks Edward over. A radio fixed to a strip of cloth on his shoulder barks. He touches it and speaks and waits. He speaks again. Light never finds his eyes. When he pushes past he says Don't go anywhere. He pulls shut the door behind him.

The old man leans to the face in the mirror. He touches the skin there. He looks in the eyes. The glare of light reflected in each. He leans in more.

Somewhere there is a knocking. He turns and then turns back. He takes a brown plastic bottle and shakes a pill into his palm and swallows it dry. He does this again. The knocking goes on. Then a door is opening and footsteps are coming. Old floor groans with each step.

"Arthur. Hey."

He turns from the mirror but his eyes dart back to find themselves one more time as he moves away.

"Arthur."

"I'm coming, yeah."

Frames line hallway walls. Comic strips from some long ago year. War posters from one side or the other, one war or the other. Edward waits by the door.

"Have they talked to you yet?"

"What?"

"Have they come by?"

"Has who come by?" "Arthur. The cops, Arthur."

He pulls open the door and the cascading blue spills in. Uniformed men move about like an anthill kicked. Now vans come, now men in plain cars. Some hold microphones and they speak into cameras. Blue-draped dragoons hold up notepads or tablets or phones. They stand talking or they stand recording or writing while others talk to them. A man in a suit, a couple in pajamas.

The couple. She talks, she looks around gesturing. He stands still, looking at the ground. A cop nods and nods.

The man in the suit talks and a cop laughs and another steps over and he laughs too. The man goes on talking. He pats pockets and reaches in and passes each cop a card. He shakes their hands.

"Bill Jack just made a sale."

The old man snorts.

"Better save the receipts, boys."

And.

"What is this?"

"John Digby is missing."

The old man looks at Edward. A moment passes. He looks again to the street.

"Do they know what happened?"

"They don't know anything."

———

Some leave and others come. Two men in suits step from a long car. They each eyeball the block and they lean close and confer. A big man in a small suit and a small man in a big suit. The big one takes out a phone and makes a call and the small one smokes. Blue wraiths wander. A man with a microphone steps over. He holds out the microphone and the small man puts a hand on it and lowers it again. He points at a house with a sign out front reading FOR SALE. The big man puts away his phone. Some minutes pass. Then they are moving squad cars and men, they are making way for a car of some luxury make. From it steps a woman of profession. Done up at this predawn hour. She talks to a cop and then another and she is ushered to the two suited men. Their talk is brief and from her they take a key, which they hand off to the officer with the square face.

The neighborhood waits. The couple are still in their pajamas. Bill Jack sits with a drink. Edward and Arthur stand watching.

Cops line the walk like troops breaking a siege. When the key turns they rush on, they disappear inside. The neighbors all lean. Somewhere there is shouting and then a full minute of nothing and when the first cop emerges every breath is held, but he comes on shaking his head, saying Not here, he's not here.

———

Their movements stall. The microphones are put away. The big man and the little man have gone. Uniforms loiter. They lean against fenders or fold sideways in their squads, booted feet on runners.

The couple cross the lawn. They each carry two cups. He hands one to Arthur, she hands one to Edward. Her fingers touch his.

"Boys. Thought you might need a coffee."

"Thank you Shane, Lauren."

"I need a whiskey," says the old man.

"We can do that too."

Edward gives a minute head shake. They sip from their cups, they talk. Questions are asked without answer. What do you think happened. Will they find him. Is he alive. More. It goes on this way. Some time later a change begins. Slow at first. Cops taking calls, a murmur passing among their ranks. Then a car pulls off, and another, and another. The gathered take note. They ask each other still more questions. What now. Did they find a body. A cop opens the door of his squad, and as he lowers himself to the seat Edward calls out.

"What's going on?"

"They got him."

"Got him? Digby?"

"No. The guy who took him."

2

The carpet is yellow and thin. Wood paneling bows on walls. A screen entombed in a cedar box plays images of a man at a lectern speaking. Tan livery and cowboy hat. Other men in cheap suits gathered. They call him the subject again and again. The subject was seen at so and so time. A dog walker in a park identified the subject. A hand goes over the microphone. The men deliberate. A man in a suit shakes his head. The uniformed man says the subject's name is Peck Algers.

Edward isn't looking. He scrolls a phone and presses the screen and scrolls again. They all talk. The town, the world.

Gossip and rumor. They say Algers was covered in blood. They say he spoke in tongues or they say he didn't speak at all. They say he confessed to killing John Jeffery Digby and half a dozen more. He's a drifter washed in from nowhere or he's a towny from an old family locked away in some attic for long years. They say all versions of maybe. The man on television goes on saying nothing.

Arthur comes into the den. He looks around and leaves again. When he returns he carries a portfolio case. Old leather cracking. He gathers pencils, he gathers notebooks.

"What are you doing, Arthur?"

"Gonna see my grandson."

He grabs keys off a table.

"You know you're not supposed to drive."

"You gonna stop me?"

"I'll drive you."

"I'll take the bus."

"Well."

Arthur sets off. Out and down the driveway and on toward the bus stop.

Edward follows but does not keep up, saying Arthur, saying Come on, Arthur. He slows and stands and the old man does not stop.

"Goddammit, Arthur."

But the words are a whisper and the old man goes on.

The vans are all gone. The cops in their squads, the newsmen, all. A truck is parked at a curb outside Bill Jack's. A man unloads boxes into Bill's garage as Bill looks on. His suit is slept in. Graying hair stands. He pays the driver in cash.

"What have you got, Bill?"

Shouted down the block.

"What do you need?"

Edward waves it off.

"I'm good, Bill."

A car turns at the corner. Little and silver and with a decade of years on it. It drives along and at the vacant it parks. It sits, engine ticking. Someone inside is moving. Little waves at nothing. A phone pans around. Then the door is opening and a woman is stepping out onto the driveway. She moves up the walk. At the door she pulls out a key. She looks around. Pale green sundress swirls as she turns. Edward raises a hand to wave but she does not see. The **FOR SALE** sign is gone.

―――

The world outside has gone and dark has come again. A car engine rises and then quiets. Somewhere a door shuts. Outside, not here. Here Edward lies in bed. A phone lights his face. His eyes move over images there. Leaked footage, the captions say. A camera watches a room. Down from a high corner. A man sits at a table. Angular face. Clothed in thick fabrics. One hand holds a coffee, the other a cigarette. He is very still. His whole being leans. A shirt and tie man enters. The man at the table animates like a doll of a man, like a wind-up toy come to life. Now he is talking but the video has no sound. He talks for some time. The shirt and tie man sits down. He lets the other man talk. The man smiles when he isn't speaking. He smiles before and after words. He puts the cigarette to his lips and talks in drifting columns. The shirt and tie man nods. The man at the table sets down his styrofoam cup. He stands from the table. The video ends.

3

Deep morning blue begins to seep in. The barest shift toward dawn. Edward rolls over and some minutes later he does so again. Then he is swinging his legs out of bed, he is leaning over his knees. Sleep is gone. He rises, he pulls on jeans. He microwaves water and stirs weak coffee. Somewhere a television tells stories he's already heard.

He sits on a porch with his mug. Sipping coffee like dirty water. The paper should come soon.

Arthur's lights are on. From somewhere an old pop song comes, but not from there. Edward watches that light, the blinds holding it in. Fingers tap on chair arm. He takes a sip.

A door opens down the block. He turns to look. A man is there in a driveway. gray suit, green tie, hair the color of straw. Shane and Lauren's house. This man moves down the drive and across the street to where a parked sedan waits. Sensible and blue. The man gets in and he starts the car and soon he is gone. Edward goes on watching long after the sedan's taillights fade. When at last he does turn away he finds Lauren's front door standing open and her in her robe. As pale morning comes on she is looking his way.

―――

Cars come and go at Bill Jack's. Edward waves as each goes by. Some wave back, some do not. Men of all stripes carrying boxes away.

Arthur's lights have not changed. Nothing has moved there. He checks a phone for the time. He stands.

Noonday sun bakes pavement. Edward crosses the street. He tries the door but it's locked. He knocks and says Arthur and knocks again. He brings out a key and has it in the aperture when the door is pulled open before him.

"What are you doing with my door?"

Arthur's shirt is untucked. His hair stands in places. He stares from the hard face of a stranger. That stare goes on for a beat, then he is softening, shoulders slumping. He does not speak but only turns and goes deeper into the house.

He points at the chair in the den. Edward sits and the old man puts on the TV and he tosses the remote and leaves the room.

"This story, huh?"

Casual now. He talks from somewhere else, voice bouncing along walls.

"You think they're gonna find him?"

"I don't know, Arthur."

"Maybe he's not even missing. Maybe he just ran off."

"May be."

When the old man comes back he brings his portfolio case.

"Going out again?"

"I gotta do something."

"Why don't you let me drive?"

"I've been going out a long time."

"Even still."

"I'll be back."

Edward follows Arthur out and down the walk to the street. The old man stops and he pats at his satchel. Edward steps near and points a few houses over.

"You see that truck at Bill's this morning?""I did not."

"Cars coming and going all day."

And.

"You know what he's doing?"

"Some damn thing."

"Maybe John Digby saw."

The old man turns a look to Edward. One eye squints hard. Mouth flat tight.

"I'll be back after a while."

He walks bent and stiff-backed along the block. Edward watches him go. He taps fingers on thigh. The road shimmers before him.

Keys on a ring are sorted. The garage key fits but the bolt is already unlocked. He rolls up its length and steps in. Corners are piled with tools and things unmade. Fans with parts strewn like guts. Tabletops lean against walls with their legs gone. An easel sits displaying a canvas gray-colored with some stain.

The car is long and old. Edges all squared. He touches the door and he pulls the handle but this is locked. He has the key for that too.

The inside smells like tobacco and earth. He closes his eyes and breathes. When he turns over the engine it simmers like a thing only just contained.

He drives slow. He's not going far. Down the block and around the corner. He parks some distance short of the bus stop.

Arthur sits on a bench. Others hover and wait. A small woman in a tracksuit, a gray man looking down. More. When the bus comes they sift in through its door and are gone.

Edward follows to the next stop. A few blocks pass by and there is another. The tracksuit woman steps out. At the next stop the gray man leaves too. Edward follows on.

At the edge of town the bus pulls off onto gravel. Men disembark from a nearby black square of building and soon pile into the bus. As they do enter Arthur steps from the bus onto ground. He goes into the place these men have just left.

Edward parks out front. There is no sign with a name, only a plastic flip card reading OPEN and a blue window neon with the name of a beer. He goes in.

Shade swallows light. Air thick with smoke squeezes each breath. He blinks and stands and in a moment he moves to the bar. A bottle sits sweating in front of Arthur. Edward points at it and orders the same and when it comes Arthur still has not spoken.

"Your grandson meeting you here?"
"I don't wanna hear it."
"I know you don't."
"Hmm."
"What are you doing later?"
"Drinking, if you'll leave."
"Come on, Arthur."
"Drunk won't make it worse."
Edward shakes his head.
"It won't make it better."
And.
"Later. What are you doing?"
"Why?"
"Come over for dinner. I'll invite people."
"There's a new one."
"A new person?"
"New neighbor."
"I saw."
"I'm sure."
"Drink your beer, Arthur."
And.
"You coming?"
"What time?"
"Later."

Arthur tips his bottle up and drinks down half in two swallows. He sets it down and touches the back of his hand to his mouth.

"Yeah," he says. "Okay."

Edward parks back on the street. He sits in the idling car, writing out a note and tearing it off and crumpling and writing again. He folds the page and crosses the street and at the house with the little silver car out front he opens the mailbox and leaves the note inside.

4

Bill Jack comes first. He says Am I first and moves past Edward. Suit loose and frayed. He carries a box with both hands. Glass thunks inside with each step. He sets the box down on a table. Places set, extra just in case. Wine, bread, jus. He lifts a bottle from the box. Square and labelless and dark. He pulls the cork and sniffs the mouth and smiles.

"You need a glass?"

"These'll work."

He pours into a wineglass, he drinks and swishes and smiles again.

"Try it. You like it, I'll get you a whole case."

"What is it?"

"I get it tax free. Truckloads of the stuff."

The doorbell rings. Edward leaves him drinking. He opens the door. Shane, Lauren. He wears a golf shirt and slacks, she's in a cocktail dress. Red, loud. She holds out a tray covered in foil.

"Are we early?"

"Bill's in the other room with some bootleg hooch he wants to sell you.

Lauren rolls her eyes. She heads that way.

"Oh, good," says Shane.

Lauren takes a call. She turns her face away to listen. She speaks hushed words. Shane drinks from a glass, neat. Shirt runs damp with sweat. He sits silent. Bill Jack drains his wineglass and refills it and drains it again. He says Where's the old Man, he says Isn't he coming.

"He said he was."

"You think he's missing?"

"What?" "Like Digby."

"I don't think he's missing."

"I think he might've done it."

"Jesus, Bill."

Bill takes a long drink from the wineglass. When he laughs drink runs from the corners of his mouth. He wipes it with a sleeve and laughs again. He says Is the new neighbor coming.

"I don't know, Bill."

He says Maybe he got her too.

Edward steps away. He pulls a door not shut but near. An office, organized, spare. Desk, computer, binders on shelves. Edward scrolls his phone, he calls Arthur. It rings. Nothing. The doorbell sounds, a loud bong that echoes. He tries the phone one more time, then steps back through the door.

Bill Jack is there. The new neighbor has come. Bill is pouring a wine glass full of dark liquor, he's talking land value, market value. How much was your house, mine cost this, I bought it way back, I got a real deal. She holds up the glass, she nods. She sees Edward and turns. His mouth is open with some unformed hello just beginning to coalesce. Then he sees they are alone.

"Where's Lauren and Shane?"

The new neighbor looks around. Bill Jack laughs wetly. He points at the front door.

They're found in the street. Shane flings out his hands and touches his face. He is there with another man. Gray suit, green tie, straw hair. Shane is not shouting but his face is hard, he speaks through teeth clenched. He steps close to the man. Lauren puts out a hand. She is shaking her head.

Somewhere there is a pop. Light comes flooding in. They all together turn. The square-faced cop is leaning from his open squad door.

"Hey. That old man belong to you?"

Edward takes a step.

"Where is he?"

"He was out walking behind town. Somebody's bringing him back."

Another pop sounds and the light fades to nothing. A front door slams and a moment later the same door opens and shuts. Down the block a sensible blue sedan comes to life and then grows distant. The cop folds back into his squad. Edward stands alone in the street.

A minute of quiet passes. Then a garage door is coming up. Edward watches Shane pull into the street and pass by gaining speed. He looks at the cop. The cop turns a hand palm up and leans back into the dark.

Lauren is there in the garage. Her arms hug her body. He stands that way, watching. Then he crosses the street and moves up the drive, he's saying Are you okay, he's saying Do you need me to call someone. She is crying in silence, shaking sobs that express some horror contained by those arms wrapped around.

"I'm not a good person."

And.

"Something is going to happen."

She reaches and presses a button and the garage door begins to fold down. He steps back to get out of its way. Soon he is alone again.

The cop has been watching. He lowers his window as Edward comes near. The cop speaks.

"Who won?"

"Were they fighting?"

"Something like that."

"Why didn't you stop them?"

The cop laughs.

"Is that you what you think my job is?"

———

The car that pulls up isn't a squad. It is black and sleek and has no markings. A woman steps out in the blue dress of these infantry and she opens the other door, she holds out a hand to steady Arthur as he stands. He takes the hand and pulls and drops it when he has found his feet. She leans to speak to him. Quiet, patient. His face turned down. He shakes his head, he closes his eyes.

Edward watches from the porch. The cop again takes Arthur's hand and she urges him on toward the house. Edward stands.

"I got him, I got him."

He jogs two steps and fast walks the rest. He pats Arthur on the back and leads him up the walk. The cop watches. She gets back in the black unmarked and goes on watching.

"Sit."

"I don't wanna sit."

"Where were you going?"

"Just going home."

"What does that mean?"

The old man shakes his head again. He breathes in hard.

"Let's get in the car," he says. "You drive."

Streetlamps sizzle as they are passed. Little worlds of light buzzing only in that space. Suburban sprawl dwindles and then stops and soon so does the housed blocks of industry and from there the light is left behind.

Country miles unspool. They run through hills and fields and past farmhouses caved in and left with their skeletal frames some decades gone. Arthur does not turn from the window. When Edward asks how far Arthur says Keep going. Swaying grasslands, fields of trees. Molding grain rolled in bails like the leavings of some now gone people, an artifact left in their hurried flight.

They are passing a wreck yard when Arthur speaks.

"There's so many now."

Rusting frames of a thousand ancient cars stretch long back into night. They age as they go, layered in eras like years sifted in earth. Windshields smashed or intact. Some taken every inch by decay, others appearing untouched.

"This lot had twenty or thirty cars. Jim Wills lived out here. His daddy plowed a dirt track for racing. They did some gambling, but he was never much good at that. But Jim started buying scrap cars up around the county, selling parts to the guys busting up their racers."

"When was all this?"

"A goddamn long time ago, Ed."

They drive in quiet for some minutes. When Arthur does speak again he says only Up here, and he points, and the car is slowing, it is turning in at a long gravel drive.

"You can just park up a ways."

The car rounds trees and follows the path and ahead in the gloom resolves a wooden farmhouse painted soft blue. Lights show in one window but the rest of the house sits in dark. Edward shuts off the engine. Night sounds come on in a rush. The scrape of insect song, the chitter of wilder things.

"Where are we, Arthur?"

"This is my grandmother's house. We moved in with her when my dad lost his job at the mine. He got another one, but we stayed a long time after that. She wanted us to. It was a safe place."

Another light comes on in the house.

"Do you want to go up? Take a look?"

"I don't want that."

And.

"She's been gone a long time."

The front door opens. The shape of a man stands silhouetted in the light of the house. The man speaks but the words are lost. Edward rolls down the window.

"You okay out here?"

Edward raises a hand.

"Took a wrong turn. We're just getting our bearings. Sorry to bother you."

The man gives a nod but he goes on watching. A minute later they back down the drive.

―――

There is no talk on the road back. The town sleeps now, the streets are empty. Like the set of a play now over and all the cast gone away. When they get to Arthur's they sit parked at the curb. The world quiet now but for the whoosh of life on the highway a mile off. There are questions unasked, unspoken thoughts and worries. The two men sit in quiet. Minutes go by.

The sound of a car grows near. Headlights turn onto the street. The car parks, the lights go out. Shane steps out, and for only a moment his eyes meet Edward's. Then he is moving, he is at his door and in. Some time later Arthur speaks.

"I'm okay," he says.
"I know you are, Arthur."

He lies still. Morning isn't far off. Television light is a flicker show on walls. Local news. A flashy story, a body found. They blur it on the network, a horror obscured, but he knows the sensible blue sedan on the screen. Through the blur he sees the green tie, the straw hair. He closes his eyes but the flicker is still there.

5

He stands in the street. He doesn't know her name. The mailbox only shows a number. He takes a step but hesitates. And now it's too late, now something changes. A car turns onto the street. It moves along and passes him by and it parks at the Digby house. He watches Angela Digby get out and go in. He follows.

His knock is gentle, polite. She answers, she says Hello. She invites him in and he says yes.

Kitchen. The lights are not on but the sun pours through long windows above a sink. He sits at a table cut from ancient stone.

"Coffee?"

He says Yes, he says Thank you. She puts a cup under a contraption and presses a button. It whirs and steams and they both watch it pour. She sets this in front of Edward and takes a seat across the table. She pulls a band from her hair. Graying locks come undone in a tumble. She speaks.

"You see the news?"

He sips from the cup.

"Which part?"

"They're letting him out."

"Algers?"

"Mmm."

"They're gonna let him out?"

"Apparently."

"He was covered in blood."

"Gossip. Who knows."

And.

"He's a weirdo but he's not the guy. Their words."

"How do you feel about it?"

"How do I feel? If he's not the guy, I don't care what he's done. I can't stop being angry right now, but he's not going to fix that."

"What about your brother?"

"What about him?"

"Are they telling you anything?"

"More gossip."

"Do you think he'll come back?"

Her sigh comes from down deep.

"I think he's just gone, Ed. And that's all there is."

She stands. She points at the cup Edward holds.

"I think I need one of those."

Another cup is set in place and the button is pressed again. Whirring, steaming.

"He was going to be mayor, you know."

She doesn't turn from the contraption. Watching the coffee come pouring out. Edward watching her. Silence.

The moment is broken by a thud and shouting. Outside but near. More shouting, a man yelling Down, down, down. Edward and Angela run to the door. Chaos has come again. Cars line the street, a van blocks egress. Cops exit Bill Jack's house. They hold him by both arms. Hands cuffed behind. He pulls against their grip, he is saying Can't a man make a living, can't a man make a living. They put him in a car and he is soon driven off.

———

They come in drifts. The pilgrims, the voyeurs, all. They come to see the show. The cops stop them at first and then they do not. They gather in the street and drink and talk. Hundreds now. They fill the block. Music plays, some forgotten pop hit, and they sway, and they talk. Someone throws a rock and they cheer, and someone throws a bottle that smashes, and now someone throws a bottle that bursts and in a kind of huff it spreads flame and they cheer again. Smoke blots a falling sun. Heat lashes at their soft bodies but still they press near. The song goes on playing.

Edward drinks from a glass. He drains it and pours another from the square and labelless bottle. He sits on the porch taking hard drinks behind the crowd as Bill Jack's house burns. Somewhere there are sirens in some other world, not here. Here there is the crowd and the fire and Edward where he sits.

He does not see her but he feels her step near.

"Can I get one of those?"

He pours another glass and she takes it in hand.

"I'm Olive," she says. "I moved in next door."

THE ROOM IN THE DESERT

The pilgrim comes upon a room in the desert. Not tall, not long, the room. A square set in blowing sands. The walls of the room are cut from slabs of solid stone. The room is laid flat, there are no rains to wash down. A door is set into one wall of the room. Old iron mounted with rivets running down and across.

The pilgrim touches the door's pull and he urges and yanks but the door does not give. He turns in place. In every direction there is desert and nothing. No landmarks, no structures, no trees, no pools. The only tracks are the pilgrim's. He touches the door again. Now the rivets, now the flat of the face. Burning with desert sun. He cups his hand, he presses an ear close, but the iron rings only with the sound of his thoughts. He bends and beneath the pull there is a keyhole but beyond this opening there is a void. He looks back the way he has come. The desert winds brush away the memory of his voyage.

The door. He again takes the pull. He braces a shoulder into the wall, and with all of him he heaves, but the door does not move. He tries to shake it, to rattle its frame. He curses and howls, but his urging and pleaing change nothing.

He sits, he waits. Hours pass. Days. His body aches and it cries out to him but still he waits, and those cries lessen and fade and he goes on waiting, and in his parched and fevered ruin he finds that he can stand, and with a sun-blackened arm he again touches the door, and he balls a fist and knocks.

"You may come in," says a soft voice from just within.

Craig Rodgers is the name appearing on several books ghostwritten by a gaggle of long dead Victorian spirits.

The following stories were previously featured in the following literary magazines:

- Partygoers, Oil on Canvas, 1672
    - The Grift - 14 Apr 2024
- At Night
    - XRAY Literary Magazine - 24 June 2019
- Odds of Life
    - Excuse Me Mag #8 - 15 Dec 2023
    - Apocalypse Confidential - STRANGE SKIES/WEIRD WORLDS special - 8 Apr 2024
- The Town's New Church
    - Apocalypse Confidential - 19 Aug 2023
- Hemingway
    - Soft Cartel - 24 June 2018
- The Latest Model
    - When Hope Writes - 31 Jan 2024
- Thomas Is a Liar
    - Soft Cartel - 7 Jan 2018
- Two Inches of Tape
    - Andromeda Spaceways #70 - Mar 2018
- Some Trouble Next Door
    - Reckon Review - 6 Nov 2023
- Whisper to Trumpet
    - Moonchild Magazine - Dec 2020
- Comes the Sorrower
    - Clash - 2018

Death of Print Titles

Consumption & Other Vices, a novel by Tyler Dempsey
Awful People, a novel by Scott Mitchel May
The Sun Still Shines on a Dog's Ass by Alan Good
Drift, a novel by Craig Rodgers
The Ghost of Mile 43, a novel by Craig Rodgers
One More Number, stories by Craig Rodgers
Francis Top's Grand Design, stories by Craig Rodgers
Detective Novel a novel by Craig Rodgers

Malarkey Books Titles

Faith, a novel by Itoro Bassey
The Life of the Party Is Harder to Find Until You're the Last One Around,
poems by Adrian Sobol
Music Is Over, a novel by Ben Arzate
Toadstones, stories by Eric Williams
Deliver Thy Pigs, a novel by Joey Hedger
It Came From the Swamp, edited by Joey Poole
Pontoon, an anthology of fiction and poetry
What I Thought of Ain't Funny,
edited by Caroljean Gavin
Guess What's Different, essays by Susan Triemert
White People on Vacation, a novel by Alex Miller
Your Favorite Poet, poems by Leigh Chadwick,
Sophomore Slump, poems by Leigh Chadwick
Man in a Cage, a novel by Patrick Nevins
Fearless, a novel by Benjamin Warner
Don Bronco's (Working Title) Shell, a novel?
by Donald Ryan
Un-ruined, a novel by Roger Vaillancourt
Thunder From a Clear Blue Sky,
a novel by Justin Bryant
Kill Radio, a novel by Lauren Bolger
The Muu-Antiques, a novel by Shome Dasgupta
Backmask, a novel by OF Cieri
Gloria Patri, a novel by Austin Ross

Where the Pavement Turns to Sand, stories by Sheldon Birnie
Still Alive, a novel by LJ Pemberton
I Blame Myself But Also You, stories by Spencer Fleury
Hope and Wild Panic, stories by Sean Ennis
Thumbsucker, poems by Kat Giordano
The Great Atlantic Highway & Other Stories, by Steve Gergley
Sleep Decades, stories by Israel A. Bonilla
First Aid for Choking Victims, stories by Matthew Zanoni Müller
Boxcutters, stories by John Chrostek
Hair Shirt, poems by Adrian Sobol
My Ardent Love for the Pencil, poems by Vi Khi Nao
The Barre Incidents, a novel by Lauren Bolger

Malarkeybooks.com

www.ingramcontent.com/pod-product-compliance
Lightning Source LLC
LaVergne TN
LVHW041621070526
838199LV00052B/3210